PAWPatrol™: PUPS SAVE THE ROYAL THRONE

A CENTUM BOOK 978-1-913110-65-9

Published in Great Britain by Centum Books Ltd

This edition published 2019

3 5 7 9 10 8 6 4 2

Centum Books Ltd, 20 Devon Square, Newton Abbot, Devon, TQ12 2HR, UK

books@centumbooksltd.co.uk

CENTUM BOOKS Limited Reg. No. 07641486

A CIP catalogue record for this book is available from the British Library.

Printed in China.

Pups Save the Royal Throne

centum

At Barkingburg Castle, the Princess is admiring her new royal throne. She's decorated it with beautiful balloons, glitter and flowers.

"One day you shall take your place on it as Queen!" says the Earl.

The Princess' pup, Sweetie, wants the throne for herself!

She suggests to the Princess that they take a photograph. When the camera flashes, there's a sudden poof of smoke!

Sweetie and her robotic toy sidekick, Buzby, float away with the throne through a secret hatch in the roof.

When the smoke clears, Sweetie and the throne have disappeared, without being seen!

"For something this important, there's only one thing we can do – call the PAW Patrol!" says the Earl.

The pups are at the Lookout when Ryder's PupPad rings.

"Someone has taken the most important treasure in Barkingburg – the royal throne!" explains the Earl.

"And my precious pup, Sweetie!" adds the Princess.

"We're on our way," replies Ryder. "No job's too big, no pup's too small!"

Ryder calls the pups to the Air Patroller.

They need to fly to Barkingburg Castle!

"PAW Patrol ready for action, Ryder, sir," says Chase.

Ryder tells the pups someone has taken the royal throne and the royal pup, Sweetie.

"An extraordinary mission like this calls for extraordinary gear," he says.

"Sounds like this is a... Mission PAW!" the pups bark.

Ryder needs Rocky to use his radar scanner to look for clues, and Skye's Sky-Cycle to scout the castle from above.

"This puppy's gotta fly!" says Skye.

"Mission PAW is on a roll!" cheers Ryder.

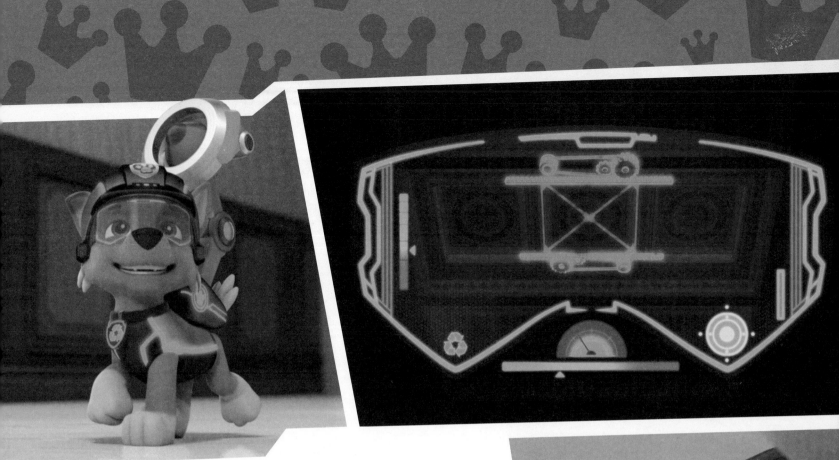

Inside the castle, Rocky rushes to the throne room to look for clues.

With his radar dish, he finds the secret panel in the ceiling.

"Maybe the throne thieves snuck out that way," says Ryder. He calls Skye and asks her to check out the roof.

Meanwhile, Sweetie and Buzby run into a problem with their escape. A crow pops the balloons on the throne with his beak, leaving it stuck on a castle turret.

Sweetie decides to change plans and hijack the Air Patroller to help her escape!

An alarm sounds on Ryder's PupPad.

"That's strange," he says. "My PupPad's telling me that the Air Patroller just took off! But who's flying it?"

Skye soars into the air in her Sky-Cycle.

"I see the throne but no sign of Sweetie," Skye radios Ryder.

Suddenly, a loud rumble fills the sky.

It's the Air Patroller... and it heads straight to the throne and scoops it up with its clamp!

Skye flies in hot pursuit of the Air Patroller and pulls up alongside the cockpit.

"Ryder, the thief is Sweetie!" says Skye.

"That's Queen Sweetie!" she replies. "Because I now have the royal throne of Barkingburg! And my autopilot Buzby is going to fly me to my very own kingdom!"

Buzby turns on the plane's hyper-speed mode, and they zoom off into the distance!

Skye joins the rest of the pups in the Mission Cruiser.

"It looks like Sweetie's headed southwest," she tells Ryder.

"If she's going that way, she's taking the Air Patroller to the jungle!" says Ryder.

Deep in the jungle, Sweetie is trying to convince the monkeys she's their new queen.

"I command you to give me all your precious gems!" she says.

But the monkeys only bring her bananas!

Just then, Queen Mandy the monkey comes out of her temple. She's a little angry that Sweetie is claiming to be queen!

When Ryder and the pups arrive, the monkeys are squabbling over the throne.

The throne bumps into a giant monkey statue, which wobbles and knocks down another statue.

Chase teams up with Tracker the Jungle Pup to stop the statues from falling onto the monkeys, but in the confusion, Sweetie makes her escape!

Ryder and the pups dash back to the Air Patroller.

"I saw the Air Patroller flying south," says Ryder,
"and I think I know where it's going!"

Sweetie lands on the ice fields and she finds a group of good-natured penguins.

"Now for my first royal command – build your beloved Queen an ice castle! The most magnificent castle ever seen in... the South Sweetie Pole!" she says.

The penguins waddle off and get to work.

Meanwhile, Jake and Everest are out penguin-watching when they see the Air Patroller.

"But where are Ryder and the PAW Patrol?" asks Everest. "I'll puptag Ryder and see what's up."

Ryder tells Everest all about Sweetie's escape with the royal throne of Barkingburg.

"Can you help us get it back?" he asks.

"Ice or snow, I'm ready to go!" says Everest.

"Rocky, it's time for some extraordinary gadget making," says Ryder. "We need a device that will take control of the Air Patroller."

"Good thing we travel with a lot of spare parts because I don't lose it, I re-use it!" Rocky yelps.

He starts preparing a plane controller!

Meanwhile, Everest has a clever idea.

"Let's push this ice chunk so it blocks Sweetie in," she whispers to Jake.

But the castle is too heavy for the ice and soon there's a loud crack!

Sweetie leaps off the throne and heads for the Air Patroller!

Marshall uses his hydro launchers to fire Rocky's plane controller onto the Air Patroller.

Rocky makes the plane spin round and round.

"Mission PAW is controlling the Air Patroller now!" Ryder radios to Sweetie.

"Okay, okay. I give up. Just stop this awful ride!" cries Sweetie.

The PAW Patrol return the throne and Sweetie to Barkingburg and join the princess for a victory photo!

"Thank you for saving the royal throne!" says the Earl.

"No problem! Whenever you have a royal problem, just say cheese for help!" cheers Ryder.

THE END